MIKE THE KNIGHT

The Amazing Egg

adapted by Cordelia Evans
based on the screenplay "Mike the Knight and Sparkie's Amazing Thing"
written by Tom Stevenson

SIMON SPOTLIGHT
An imprint of Simon & Schuster Children's Publishing Division
New York London Toronto Sydney New Delhi
1230 Avenue of the Americas, New York, New York 10020

For information about special discounts for bulk purchases, please contact
Simon & Schuster Special Sales at 1-866-506-1949 or business@simonandschuster.com.
Manufactured in China 1013 LEO
First Edition 2 4 6 8 10 9 7 5 3 1
ISBN 978-1-4424-9549-4

It was the day of the Glendragon Show-and-Tell, and everyone in the village was busy preparing for the big show.

"There! Those are some of the best horseshoes I've ever made," said Mr. Blacksmith as he finished fitting shiny new horseshoes onto Galahad's hooves.

"Now he's ready for my show-and-tell," said Mike.

"It looks like Evie is getting ready too," Sparkie said, pointing across the way. Evie waved her wand and chanted a magic spell. As usual, her magic didn't go as planned.

Mike worried that his show-and-tell wouldn't be as amazing as everybody else's.

"But, Mike, you're going to show all your amazing knightly things!" encouraged Sparkie.

"You're right, Sparkie!" cried Mike. "I'm Mike the Knight, and my mission is . . . to amaze everyone with my knightly show-and-tell."

Mike raced off to his bedroom to put on his armor.

Then Mike slid down to the stable. He hopped on Galahad and went to draw his sword. He pulled out . . .

"*I've* got an amazing thing for your show, Mike," announced Squirt as they left the castle and walked to the village.

"Me too, Mike!" said Sparkie.

"Okay!" said Mike. "You're my dragons, so your amazing things should be in my show-and-tell."

Squirt's amazing thing was . . .

"Wow, Squirt!" said Mike. "Your grandfather must have been one of the biggest dragons ever! That tooth is going right at the front of my show-and-tell."

He turned to Sparkie. "What's your amazing thing, Sparkie?"

Sparkie proudly held out his amazing thing, which was . . .

Mike was worried. Sparkie's egg didn't look very amazing—or knightly.

"Maybe we should put it backstage," he whispered to Squirt. He carefully picked up the egg and placed it behind the curtain.

Soon the audience arrived and it was time for Mike's show-and-tell. His archery trophy, bow and arrow, and Squirt's grandfather's tooth were proudly displayed up on the stage. Squirt blew on a trumpet to signal that the show was about to begin. Mike and Galahad galloped into the theater. Meanwhile, backstage . . .

When Sparkie came looking for his amazing egg, it was gone!

"Where's my amazing egg?" he cried, coming out on stage and interrupting Mike's show-and-tell.

Sparkie ran through the audience looking for his egg.

Then he ran through the village and ruined Mrs. Piecrust's show-and-tell.

"Thank you, Mike!" said Sparkie. "And it's almost time for the surprise!"

They brought the egg back to the stage just in time to see it burst open, letting out streams of light. Out flew . . .